E
SW

Swope, Sam

The Araboolies of
Liberty Street

$14.99

DATE			

F

To Trevor
S.M.S.

In memory of my brother Steve
B.R.

the ARABOOLIES
of LIBERTY STREET

story by SAM SWOPE   pictures by BARRY ROOT

Clarkson N. Potter, Inc./Publishers

nce there was a street called Liberty Street, and Liberty Street was lined with white houses that were so much alike it was difficult to tell one from another. This was just the way fat General Pinch and his skinny wife liked it.

The Pinches spied on their neighbors all day long. They had nothing better to do. They hated anything that looked like fun. They got upset when Joy hung upside down from a maple tree. They got angry when Katie crept around like a tiger. They got *furious* when Jack spun around until he felt dizzy. And whenever the Pinches got upset, or angry, or *furious*, the General would grab his bullhorn and shout "I'll call in the army!" and the fun would have to stop, right then and there.

When summer came, the Pinches ordered the children to stay inside.

The kids were miserable. So were their parents, but what could they do? Everyone was terrified of the General and his army, and orders were orders: the children had to stay inside.

It was a lonely time.

General and Mrs. Pinch smiled nasty smiles and stood proudly at their windows, keeping a sharp lookout for fresh trouble—tulips growing, robins building nests, that kind of thing. And whenever the Pinches saw anything they didn't like, the General would haul out his bullhorn. "I'll call in the army!" he'd holler.

Liberty Street was certainly clean and quiet—you had to give the Pinches credit for that. But you never heard any music or laughter there, or saw any toys or happy children. It was a sad place, and that made the Pinches very glad.

Then one day the Araboolies came to Liberty Street and moved in next door to the Pinches. They gave the General and his wife a lot to look at.

For one thing, there were dozens and dozens of them: children and moms and dads and aunts and uncles and grandparents and great-grandparents and great-great-great-grandparents. For another, the Araboolies had pets. They had anteaters and porcupines. Elephants, walruses and sloths. They even had a wok, a few popaloks and a wild barumpuss!

Mrs. Pinch sucked in both cheeks. "Disgusting!" she hissed.

"I'll call in the army!" boomed the General.

But that didn't bother the Araboolies. They didn't speak English. They didn't know *what* those Pinches were screaming about.

Now, the Araboolies came from an island far away where people are born with colorful skin. Strangely enough, however, the Araboolies were never the same color from one day to the next. For example, one day Grandfather Araboolie might be orange, Auntie Araboolie blue, and Baby Araboolie pink. But Gramps could just as easily have woken up yellow, Auntie green, and Baby purple. You just never knew.

At night, the Araboolies glowed in the dark.
"Revolting!" squawked Mrs. Pinch, stomping her feet.
"I'll call in the army!" bellowed the General.
The first improvement the Araboolies made to their home was to paint
it with red and white zigzags. They decorated it with flashing colored lights and
hung toys from the trees. Then they drew jungle scenes on the sidewalks and
poured sand on the grass and made sand creatures.

The Araboolies weren't the neatest people in the world, truth to tell, but they sure knew how to have fun. They put their furniture all over the yard and lived outside—they played outside, ate outside and watched TV outside. The Araboolies even *slept* outside, all cuddled up like puppies in the biggest bed you ever saw in your life. They snored like crazy!

The animals lived inside—in the shower, in the sink, under the stairs and in the chimney. They ran all over the place! What a racket they made!

"No noise!" screeched Mrs. Pinch, shaking her bony fists in the air.
And you can guess what the General hollered.

But no matter how much the Pinches screamed, the Araboolies didn't pay any attention. They were having too much fun.

General and Mrs. Pinch were miserable. All this happiness was making them sick. Things were getting out of control! Why, before they knew it *all* the children

of Liberty Street were outside playing boolanoola ball!

"This has got to stop!" shrieked Mrs. Pinch, her eyes popping out of her head.

Just then, Joy clobbered the boolanoola ball. It went up and up and up until—
oh, no!—it crashed through the Pinches' window and smashed into the General's
stomach—pow!—and knocked him flat!

"Ouch!" roared the General.

The Pinches were out in a flash.

"This means war!" wailed Mrs. Pinch.

"I'll call in the army!" cried the General, and he whipped out his walkie-talkie. "Come in, army!" he thundered. "Attack Liberty Street at dawn!"

Then the Pinches stormed home and slammed the door—but not before their cat Naomi had escaped and gone to the Araboolies' house to live.

The Araboolies smiled and shrugged, but the rest of Liberty Street was in a panic. The army was coming! Doors were locked and blinds were pulled down tight. Everyone was terrified!

Everyone, that is, but Joy. "Those mean old Pinches," she thought. "When their army comes, they'll take away the Araboolies. Well, I won't let them! I won't!"

And so she thought and thought and thought until she had an idea.

She waited until night came. And then, when the parents of Liberty Street were asleep, Joy tiptoed outside and sneaked around Liberty Street, waking the other children and telling them her plan. "What a neat idea!" they said.

Because there wasn't a moment to lose, they all got busy right away. But they

had to be very quiet so their parents wouldn't wake up. The children crept down to their basements and up to their attics. They dug through closets and drawers. They gathered together toys and balloons and finger paints. They rounded up scissors and wrapping paper and they pulled out decorations from Christmas, Thanksgiving and Halloween. Then they went outside.

Some of the children colored the houses and pasted animal cut-outs in the windows. Others decorated the trees and painted the sidewalks. They put toys everywhere and dragged furniture outside. They worked all night long. The last thing they did was to paint one another's faces.

The Araboolies snored through it all.

It was almost dawn when they were finished. Liberty Street had never ever looked wilder or more colorful, and the children were very proud.

Before long, they heard the angry rumble of the army approaching. The ground shook. Soon there were guns and bombs and helicopters and thousands of soldiers marching past the colorful homes of Liberty Street.

Now, armies, of course, don't think. They only follow orders. And General Pinch's orders were very clear. "There's a house on Liberty Street that's different!" he roared from his window. "It's disgusting! Get rid of it! And get rid of the weirdos who live in it!"

And so, with those orders in mind, the soldiers marched up Liberty Street. But all they saw were brightly painted homes and colorful people. No house was different. No one was weird. The soldiers didn't know what to do.

But when they finally reached the end of Liberty Street—there it was! A different house, plain and white, with a fat angry man and a nasty skinny woman inside. "That's them!" shouted the army. "They're the weirdos!"

"Charge!" ordered the General.

And the army did just that. The soldiers surrounded the house and tied it up with ropes. "Not us, you idiots!" squealed Mrs. Pinch.

"I'll call in the army!" cried the General.

But the army was already there, following orders.

And so it was that the Pinches and their house were yanked from the ground and dragged far, far away, as the children cheered and the Araboolies waved good-bye. And the terrible Pinches were never seen on Liberty Street ever again.

The End

Text copyright © 1989 by Samuel Swope
Illustrations copyright © 1989 by Barrett Root

Published by Clarkson N. Potter, Inc., 225 Park Avenue South, New York, New York 10003,
and distributed by Crown Publishers, Inc.

CLARKSON N. POTTER, POTTER, and colophon are trademarks of Clarkson N. Potter, Inc.

Manufactured in Hong Kong

Library of Congress Cataloging-in-Publication Data
Swope, Samuel.
The Araboolies of Liberty Street/story by Sam Swope; pictures by Barry Root.
Summary: The kids of Liberty Street join forces to help the Araboolies when mean General Pinch orders them to move because they look different.
[1. Toleration—Fiction.]   I. Root, Barry, ill.   II. Title.
PZ7.S9826Ar   1988
[E]—dc19   88-12687
ISBN 0-517-56960-4
ISBN 0-517-57411-X (lib. bdg.)
10 9 8 7 6 5 4 3 2 1

First Edition